Chapter 1

A Visit to Aunty Jess

Cherry Bakewell went into her daughter's bedroom, "Good morning Peaches. It's time to get up."

"Morning mummy. What are we doing today?"

"Aunty Jess isn't feeling very well, so I thought we would take her some soup," replied Cherry.

"Can I help mummy?" said Peaches.

"Of course. Go and get ready and I'll get your breakfast," said Cherry.

Peaches got out of bed and looked outside. The weather looked a bit sad because it was raining.

"Oh dear, maybe a giant is crying," she said.

She got ready and went downstairs. Cherry gave Peaches some toast with jam and orange juice.

As Peaches ate her breakfast she asked, "How do we make soup mummy?"

Cherry went to the book shelf. "I'll get The Big Green Cookery book." She opened the book at Carrot and Parsnip soup. "This will be perfect. We need onion, celery, garlic, parsnips, carrots, butter, sunflower oil, a vegetable stock cube, water and salt and pepper," she read out loud.

Together they collected all the ingredients and put them on the table.

"If you peel the carrots and parsnips Peaches, I'll chop the onion, celery and garlic," said Cherry.

"Ok mummy," she said as she picked up the vegetable peeler. As Cherry started to chop the onions, she had tears running down her face. "Mummy, why are you crying?" asked Peaches.

"The onions always make me cry," sniffed Cherry.

"I think a giant must have been sad earlier as there were tears coming out of the clouds." said Peaches.

Cherry laughed, "Ha ha! That's only the rain," she chuckled.

After the carrots and parsnips had been peeled, Cherry chopped them up quite small so they cooked quicker.

"There we are, ready to start," she said cheerfully.

She put the butter and oil in the pan, then added the onion, celery and garlic. Peaches began to stir, cooking them for about ten minutes until they were soft.

"Now we add the carrots and parsnips," instructed Cherry. Then she added the stock and salt and pepper. "We need to cook the vegetables for about fifteen minutes until they are soft, then we put it in the blender."

"It smells nice mummy," smiled Peaches. "I'm sure Aunty Jess will love it."

After fifteen minutes, Cherry put the soup in the blender adding a little at a time so it didn't spill out. Round and round it went, making a lovely orange-coloured soup. When it was all done, she poured it into a flask.

"We can have the rest for lunch when we come back," she suggested.

"Ooh I can't wait," said Peaches.

They packed the soup in the car and drove to Aunty Jess's house. Peaches ran up the garden path and Aunty Jess came to the door.

"Hello my lovely," she said.

"Hello Aunty Jess," said Peaches excitedly. "We've made you some soup as mummy said you weren't very well."

"That's right, I have a bad cold, so that soup will go down a treat. Thank you," said Aunty Jess. Peaches gave her a hug.

"Can I come and see Cornflake?" asked Peaches.

"Yes, of course, he's in the front room," said Aunty Jess.

Cornflake was Aunty Jess's hamster and he was poking his nose though the bars of the cage. She gave him a cuddle and Cherry warmed the soup and made some tea.

"I hope the soup makes you feel better Aunty Jess," said Peaches.

"I'm sure it will," smiled Aunty Jess.

After about an hour, it was time to go home. Aunty Jess had loved their visit and started to feel much better. They kissed her goodbye and got in the car.

As they drove home, Peaches said, "I enjoyed that mummy. Can we do some more cooking?"

"Definitely," replied Cherry Bakewell. "I wonder what tomorrow will bring?"

Carrot and Parsnip Soup

1 onion, 3 celery stalks, 1 clove of garlic, 2 large parsnips,
2 large carrots, 25g butter, 1 tablespoon sunflower oil,
1 vegetable stock cube, 1 litre of boiling water, salt and pepper

1. Peel the parsnips and carrots and chop into small pieces.
2. Chop onion, celery and garlic and cook in a pan with the oil and butter for about 10 minutes until soft.
3. Add the carrots and parsnips.
4. Make the vegetable stock with the water and add to the pan with a little salt and pepper to taste. Cook for 10-15 minutes until the vegetables are soft, stirring occasionally.
5. Place a little in a blender at a time, and blend until smooth.

Chapter 2

Mushroom Picking

Cherry Bakewell and Peaches had just eaten their tea and Peaches was doing her homework. "Do you fancy picking some mushrooms tomorrow Peaches?" asked Cherry.

"Yes, please mummy," she replied.

"We need to get up early, about 6.00 o'clock. I have a lovely recipe for lunch tomorrow," said Cherry.

After about an hour, Peaches had finished her homework.

"Right young lady, it's time for bed," said Cherry. "Set your alarm and get a good night's sleep."

"Okay mummy," replied Peaches.

She gave Nippy a big hug then went upstairs. As she climbed into bed, she thought to herself, Wow! 6 o'clock. That's early! I'd better get to sleep." She snuggled down in her warm and cosy bed.

The next morning, Peaches was ready early and went running downstairs.

"I'm ready mummy," exclaimed Peaches.

"Hello sweetheart," said Cherry. "We'll have breakfast when we come home as it's still a bit early."

"Okay, can we take Nippy?" asked Peaches.

"Yes, said Cherry, put his lead on and we'll get going."

As they walked up to the woods, they took Nippy's lead off as he loved running and jumping around in the leaves!

"We need to look for fairy rings Peaches," said Cherry.

"What are they mummy?" Peaches asked.

"It's a patch of dark grass in a circle. The mushrooms grow around the outside."

Finally, they found one, and lo and behold, there were mushrooms growing around the outside.

"You have to know which mushrooms to pick Peaches as some of them are poisonous. These are perfect!" exclaimed Cherry. Peaches bent down and put the mushrooms in her basket.

"What are we making mummy?" Peaches enquired.

"I have a lovely recipe for cheesy rainbow vegetables with ham," replied Cherry.

"Ooh, that sounds yummy!" Peaches said. They hurried home as their tummies were rumbling and they needed their breakfast!

When they arrived home, Peaches had some cereal and juice and asked, "When are we making lunch mummy?

"Ha ha! You've only just had your breakfast," said Cherry. Go and play for a while and I'll call you when I'm ready."

Peaches went into the garden to play with Nippy. She threw the football and he jumped up and caught it in his paws!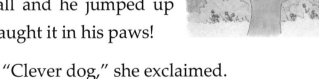

"Clever dog," she exclaimed.

After some time, Cherry called out, "Peaches, can you come in and wash your hands?"

"Coming mummy," she replied. She washed and dried her hands and went to get The Big Green Cookery Book and opened it at the recipe.

 Cherry had washed all the vegetables and put everything on the table. There were red and yellow peppers, courgettes, butternut squash, red onion, the mushrooms they had picked, paprika, garlic, thyme, sunflower oil, spring onions, ham, butter, flour, milk, mature cheddar cheese and parmesan cheese.

"Wow!" exclaimed Peaches, "I love all these colours!"

"Peaches, could you slice the courgette and mushrooms and I'll chop the peppers, onion and the butternut squash?" asked Cherry.

"Alright mummy," she said.

They put everything into a large dish and mixed it up.

"It looks just like a rainbow mummy," said Peaches.

"Yes, don't they look nice?" said Cherry and added the paprika, garlic, thyme, and one tablespoon of sunflower oil. "They need to roast for fifty minutes. You can do some colouring while they're cooking if you want?" said Cherry.

"Okay," said Peaches.

Cherry made the sauce by melting the butter in the pan, adding flour to make a paste, then pouring in some milk, a little at a time. She added some of the cheese and the parmesan. As she was stirring, she asked Peaches, "Would you chop some spring onions and ham for me lovey?"

"Yes mummy," she said.

Cherry took the vegetables out of the oven, sprinkled on the ham and poured over the cheese sauce. Peaches added the rest of the cheese and spring onions to the top and Cherry put it back in the oven to brown. As it was cooking, Peaches looked through the glass door of the oven.

"It smells really nice mummy and it's all bubbly," she said excitedly.

Peaches helped her mum set the table with a red tablecloth, knives and forks and some glasses of squash, then sat down to wait. Cherry brought it to the table and they both tucked into their lunch.

"Ooh mummy, it tastes lovely! I didn't know rainbows tasted so good!"

That afternoon Peaches was sat on the sofa doing her colouring and it wasn't long before she had fallen asleep with Nippy lying next to her.

Cherry looked over and said, "Oh bless, they've both had a busy day!"

Cheesy Rainbow Vegetables and Ham

1 red pepper and 1 yellow pepper, cut into chunks,
1 courgette, sliced, ½ butternut squash, cut into cubes,
1 red onion, chopped, 150g closed cup mushrooms, sliced,
1 tsp paprika, 1 clove garlic, crushed, 1 sprig of thyme,
1 tablespoon sunflower oil, 4 chopped spring onions,
200g ham, chopped, 30g butter, 1 tablespoon plain flour,
½ pint milk, 140g mature cheddar cheese,
55g grated parmesan, salt and pepper to taste

1. Place the vegetables in a large ovenproof dish and sprinkle with paprika, garlic, thyme leaves pulled off the stalk and sunflower oil and mix through. Cook for 50 minutes on gas 6, 200 degrees C, stirring occasionally
2. Melt the butter in a saucepan add the flour, then whisk in the milk. Add 85g cheese, parmesan, salt and pepper to taste and cook for a couple of minutes until smooth.
3. Sprinkle the ham over the vegetables, pour over the cheese sauce and sprinkle the top with the other 55g of cheese and spring onions. Bake for a further 20 minutes until bubbling.

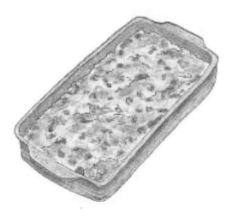

Chapter 3

Honey Bees

It was a lovely sunny day and Peaches was in the classroom at school learning all about bees and how they make honey. The teacher, Miss Rose, was drawing a picture on the board.

"The bees take the nectar, which is a sweet sugary juice, from the flowers by sucking it with their tongues. They store it in what is called their honey stomach. When they have had enough, they fly back to the hive where it is given to the worker bees to make honey. Maybe you could all draw a picture of a bee?" said Miss Rose. The children settled down with paper and pencils and drew their bees.

The bell went for lunch and the children sat outside in the sunshine. As Peaches was eating her lunch, she saw some bees flying around the flowers.

"Those bees work so hard," she thought to herself.

Cherry Bakewell was at home doing some sewing on her sewing machine. She loved making things. She was making some squares of material which she was going to fill with lavender and hang in the wardrobes to make the clothes smell nice.

"I wonder what to make for dinner tonight? Maybe Peaches can help me decide," she thought.

She finished what she was doing and said "Nippy, let's go for a quick walk before we pick Peaches up from school." He came bounding across the floor excitedly, wagging his tail, nearly knocking Cherry over! He did like his walks.

As they came up to the woods, hiding behind a bush was a

 naughty little racoon, called Rickster Raccoon. He would sneak up behind people and jump out to scare them. When Cherry was baking, he would try and pinch the food. He was always in trouble. He walked around wearing shades. He thought he was very cool!

"I can see you Rickster. You stay away from my kitchen," said Cherry.

As she walked away, he gave a cheeky laugh. Who knows what he will get up to next! Before long, it was time to pick up Peaches from school. Cherry parked the car and went into the playground to get her daughter.

"Hello mummy, we've been learning about honey bees today," she said excitedly, and showed Cherry her picture of a bee.

"Oh, that's interesting. That's given me an idea for dinner. I have a recipe for honey and ginger chicken," replied Cherry.

"That sounds nice Mummy, can we make it?" asked Peaches.

"Yes, it doesn't take long. As it's warm, we can have it with a nice salad," said Cherry.

When they arrived home, Peaches got The Big Green Cookery Book down from the shelf.

"Here it is mummy, page nine," said Peaches.

Cherry got all the ingredients together and put them on the table.

"We have to make a marinade to put on the chicken and leave it in the fridge for about forty-five minutes," exclaimed Cherry.

"What's a marinade?" asked Peaches.

"It's like a sauce which covers the meat and gives it flavour," replied Cherry.

"Can you put the soy sauce and honey in a bowl please Peaches?"

"Okay mummy," replied Peaches.

"Then, can you add the Dijon mustard, water and ground ginger and I'll crush the garlic?" asked Cherry.

"Okay, that sounds tasty mummy," answered Peaches.

Cherry added some pepper to the other ingredients in the bowl, then added the chicken and put it in the fridge for forty-five minutes.

"Now we'll chop the salad," said Cherry.

"Okay, but no tomato!" exclaimed Peaches.

"No, I know you don't like tomatoes!" said Cherry.

They sliced and chopped lettuce, cucumber, red pepper and spring onions and added sweetcorn until they had a nice bowl of salad. After forty-five minutes, Cherry took the chicken out of the fridge and cooked it on the griddle pan for four or five minutes per side, then sliced it up and put it on the salad.

"Let's go and eat outside as it's sunny," said Cherry.

"Ooh yes please," said Peaches.

They settled down at the garden table.

"Wow, that's nice mummy," exclaimed Peaches.

"It's nice, isn't it and so healthy," replied Cherry.

As they were eating dinner, Peaches noticed the bees on the flowers.

"Look mummy, the bees are working hard again. Thank you, bees, for making our honey," she said. "Our dinner was yummy!" Cherry looked on and smiled.

Honey and Ginger Chicken

2 chicken breasts, 2 tablespoons honey, 2 tablespoons soy sauce,
2 cloves garlic, 1 teaspoon Dijon mustard, 4 tablespoons water,
2 tsp ground ginger, pepper to taste

Salad

Lettuce, cucumber, 1 small tin sweetcorn, 1 red pepper,
6 spring onions

1. Put the honey, soy sauce, garlic, mustard, water, ginger and pepper in a bowl and mix thoroughly.
2. Add the chicken. Cover and put it in the fridge for 45 minutes.
3. Chop the lettuce, red pepper and spring onions and place into a bowl and add some cucumber slices and tinned sweetcorn.
4. Remove the chicken from the fridge and cook on the griddle pan for 4-5 minutes per side. Slice and place on top of the salad.

Chapter 4

Aunty Jean's Birthday

It was Saturday morning and Peaches was in the garden playing with Nippy. He was running around in circles trying to catch his tail.

"Ha ha! You're so funny Nippy!" laughed Peaches.

Then came a call from the house.

"Peaches can you come in, we need to go to the shops," shouted Cherry.

"Coming mummy," replied Peaches.

As she got to the house Cherry said, "It's Aunty Jean's birthday today, so we need to get her some flowers and make her a cake and I also need some flour."

"Oh good. It will be nice to see Aunty Jean," said Peaches.

They picked up their bag and opened the front door.

"Nippy will have to sit at home this time. Mr. Hoskins doesn't allow dogs in the shop. He'll probably have a sleep," said Cherry.

"Bye Nippy, have a nice sleep," whispered Peaches.

They arrived at Mr. Hoskins' shop and there were lots of bunches of flowers. Peaches picked up red carnations and purple freesias.

"Ooh! Freesias smell so lovely! Aunty Jean will love them," exclaimed Cherry.

They took them into the shop and also picked up the bag of flour that Cherry needed.

"Good morning Mr. Hoskins," said Peaches. "We're making my Aunty Jean a birthday cake."

"Oh, that's nice, wish her a happy birthday from me," said Mr. Hoskins.

"Okay, I will," said Peaches.

When they arrived home, they opened The Big Green Cookery Book.

"Peaches would you weigh the margarine, castor sugar and self-raising flour and put them in the bowl?"

"Yes, I can do that," said Peaches.

Cherry cracked eggs into the bowl with baking powder and vanilla extract.

"That's it, now we add a splash of milk," said Cherry.

She whisked the cake until it was light and fluffy, then divided it between two eight-inch sandwich tins and cooked it for twenty-five minutes. When it was ready, she put it on a cooling rack. Cherry made the buttercream by mixing the butter and icing sugar in a bowl with the vanilla extract.

"While its cooling Peaches, would you like to make Aunty Jean a card?" asked Cherry. "Yes, please mummy, can I use glitter?" said Peaches excitedly. "Yes, but put lots of newspaper down as the glitter goes everywhere!" replied Cherry.

Peaches drew a flower and wrote Happy Birthday, then got her glue stick and started putting glitter on, lots and lots of glitter!

Nippy came to have a look and got glitter all over his nose!

"Oh no, you're a very sparkly dog now," laughed Cherry.

After Peaches had finished, Cherry said "Go and wash your hands then we can finish the cake."

"Okay mummy," replied Peaches.

Cherry and Peaches spread the buttercream and then the jam on the bottom cake, then placed the other cake on top. Peaches sprinkled icing sugar on the top. All of a  sudden, they heard a crash! It was that naughty Rickster Raccoon! Oh no! He had crept in the door and was pinching some chocolate from the store cupboard.

"Rickster! Get out of my kitchen," shouted Cherry and he ran down the road with chocolate all round his face, laughing to himself.

"He is so naughty!" exclaimed Peaches.

They picked up the chocolate and tidied up. They never knew what he would get up to next!

That afternoon, they arrived at Aunty Jean's house.

"Happy Birthday Aunty Jean," shouted Peaches and gave her a hug and her presents.

"What beautiful flowers and a lovely cake as well, thank you!" exclaimed Aunty Jean. "Let's have a slice of cake and a cup of tea," suggested Aunty Jean.

Peaches gave her Aunty the sparkly card and lots of glitter fell onto the floor. "Ha ha!" said Aunty Jean. "You certainly have made my birthday sparkle!"

Victoria Sponge

Cake

225g soft margarine, 225g castor sugar, 4 eggs
225g self-raising flour, 1½ level teaspoons baking powder
1 teaspoon vanilla extract, Splash of milk

Filling

50g softened butter, 75g icing sugar,
1 teaspoon vanilla extract, 2 tablespoons strawberry jam
A little icing sugar to sprinkle on top.

1. Put all the cake ingredients in a bowl and mix with an electric whisk until light and fluffy.
2. Divide the mixture between 2 x 8-inch round sandwich tins lined with non-stick cake liners and bake for 25 minutes on gas 5, 190°C.
3. Mix the butter, icing sugar, and vanilla extract together until smooth. When the cake is cool, spread with the buttercream on one half, then the jam and place the second cake on top.
4. Sprinkle with icing sugar.

Chapter 5

Family Reunion

School had finished for the holidays and Peaches was lying in bed. She suddenly got really excited.

"Daddy and Freddie are coming home today," she thought.

Her Daddy was the Captain of a ship and was away for a couple of weeks at a time, but was due home today. Freddie was her brother and had been on a school trip camping in France. She ran downstairs full of excitement.

"Mummy, can we make Daddy and Freddie some apricot and pecan cookies?" she said.

"Yes, that will be nice. Let's see if we have all the ingredients," said Cherry.

She looked in the cupboard to check.

"Oh no, we've run out of dried apricots. Let's pop down to Mr. Hoskins and get some," she said. They drove down to the shops.

"Morning Mr. Hoskins, my Daddy and Freddie are coming home today and we're making them some cookies," said Peaches.

"Oh, how exciting. Happy baking!" said Mr. Hoskins. They paid for the apricots and drove home.

 Back at the house, that naughty Rickster Raccoon was hiding in the bushes. As they walked up the path, he jumped out and said "SURPRISE!" Cherry jumped so much that she nearly dropped the apricots!

"Rickster, you are so naughty!" said Peaches and he ran off down the road, laughing to himself.

In the kitchen, Peaches found the recipe in The Big Green Cookery Book. She put everything on the table.

"Right," said Cherry. "We need to mix the butter and brown sugar together."

Peaches whisked them until they were light and fluffy, then Cherry added an egg and Peaches mixed it again.

"Next we add flour, vanilla, bicarbonate of soda, chopped pecans and apricots and mix again," said Cherry.

She covered the bowl in clingfilm and put it in the fridge.

"We'll cook them later on," she said.

"Okay, can I play in the garden?" said Peaches.

"Yes, Daddy will be home about twelve o'clock," said Cherry.

"Okay," said Peaches.

She was playing tug-of-war with Nippy and an old rope, and was laughing so much that she fell onto the grass and Nippy jumped on top of her, wagging his tail.

"Oh Nippy!   You do make me laugh," she giggled.

After about an hour, a call came from the kitchen.

"Where's my girl then?" said a man's voice. She ran into the kitchen to see her daddy, Jack Bakewell.

"Daddy! I've missed you," she said excitedly.

"I've missed you too," said Jack. "I have a present for you Peaches," and he pulled a parcel out of his bag.

Peaches opened it up to find a kaleidoscope. It was a long tube that made pictures when you looked through it.

"Oh, I love it." exclaimed Peaches.

After a little while, Cherry said, "Come on Peaches, we need to pick up Freddie from his school trip."

"Okay mummy," said Peaches. Off they went to the school, both feeling excited.

They waited in the car park for about five minutes, then they saw the bus coming around the corner.

"He's here!" said Peaches.

They could see Freddie waving out of the bus window. Peaches got out of the car with Cherry and they went to meet him.

"Freddie!" cried Peaches and she gave him a big hug.

"Hi Freddie, did you have a good time?" asked Cherry.

"Brilliant! We built fires, made rafts and sang around the campfire," explained Freddie excitedly.

"Sounds like fun!" said Cherry.

As they drove home, Freddie was telling stories of his trip, how they toasted marshmallows on the fire and had to find their way through the woods with a compass. Once they were home, he saw his dad waiting for him.

"Hiya dad," he said.

"Alright mate? Good time was it?" said Jack.

"Yeah, brill, I made a raft and fell in the water!" said Freddie. "Ha ha! I bet that was fun!" laughed Jack.

Cherry got the cookie mixture out of the fridge and put scoops onto a baking tray and cooked them for about twelve to fifteen minutes. Freddie and Peaches were playing with Nippy and the smell of the cookies was filling the kitchen. Then the timer went off and everyone came rushing over to have a look at the cookies, including Nippy! He was bouncing up and down hoping to get one! They all sat down eating, chatting and laughing. It was so nice to have the family back together again.

Apricot and Pecan Cookies

120g butter, 200g light muscovado sugar, 1 egg,
1 tsp vanilla extract, 240g plain flour, ½ tsp bicarbonate of soda,
145g chopped dried apricots, 65g chopped pecans

1. Cream the butter and sugar together until light and fluffy, add the egg and mix again.
2. Add rest of ingredients and mix thoroughly.
3. Cover in clingfilm and put in the fridge for about an hour.
4. Using an ice cream scoop, put scoops of the mixture on a baking tray lined with parchment about 2 inches apart and bake for about 12-15 minutes on gas 5, 190°C. Cool on a wire rack.

Chapter 6

A Trip to the Beach

It was a beautiful sunny day and Cherry, Jack, Freddie and Peaches were sitting eating their breakfast.

"As it's a nice day and we're back together, how about we pack up a picnic and go the beach?" said Cherry.

"Ooh yes," said Freddie, "I'll take my kite and ball."

"I'll make some orange and cranberry cupcakes to take with us, do you two want to help?" asked Cherry.

"Yes please," replied Freddie and Peaches.

Freddie got The Big Green Cookery Book to see what was

needed. He opened the book at the recipe.

"We need margarine, castor sugar, eggs, self-raising flour, baking powder, two oranges, dried cranberries, orange extract and icing sugar."

Cherry, Peaches and Freddie collected up all the ingredients and put them on the table ready to start baking.

"Peaches could you weigh the margarine and castor sugar into a bowl please?"

"Okay mummy," she said.

"I'll crack the eggs and Freddie, could you measure out the flour and baking powder for me?"

"Okay mum," said Freddie.

When everything was in the bowl, Freddie whisked it until it was all blended together.

"Now we need to add orange zest and juice and a little orange extract. Peaches, could you measure the cranberries for me please? Mix them with a little flour, it stops them from sinking."

"Okay mummy," she said. Peaches mixed it up, scooped them into paper cases and baked them for twenty minutes.

"Right kids, while they're cooking, get your things together," said Jack.

"Okay dad," said Freddie.

He picked up his kite and football and put them in the car. Peaches grabbed her bucket and spade and a couple of blankets.

"I've got your swimming costumes if you want a paddle, and some towels," said Cherry.

She made some sandwiches and squash with some water for Nippy. After twenty minutes, the timer went off.

"They're ready mummy," cried Peaches.

"Okay, lovely," replied Cherry.

She had made some orange icing with icing sugar, orange juice and orange extract, which she put on the cupcakes when they were cool, then sprinkled them with grated orange rind and dried cranberries. She put them in a box and they all set off for the beach.

On the journey, Nippy had his head out of the window to keep cool and Freddie and Peaches were playing I-spy.

"I spy with my little eye, something beginning with S," said Peaches.

"Steering wheel," said Freddie.

"Nope," said Peaches. "It's the sea, we're here!" she said excitedly.

"Yeah", said Freddie.

Jack parked up and Cherry put the blankets down and put up a windbreak for some shelter. Peaches and Freddie changed into their costumes with dad holding the towel.

"I'll race you," said Freddie.

They ran towards the sea with Nippy following on behind. They laughed and splashed and Nippy kept trying to jump on top of the waves to catch them. After a little while, Cherry called them.

"Come on you two, time for food," she shouted.

They came running up the beach, grabbed a towel and got themselves dry before sitting down for lunch.

Then came Nippy, all wet.

"Oh no, don't you shake," said Cherry, but too late, he shook so much, it was as if it was raining!"

"Oh Nippy, you've made me all wet again!" said Peaches. Cherry and Jack sat there laughing.

They had ham sandwiches and egg and cress.

"Phew! Stinky egg!" said Freddie.

"Ha ha! I know you don't like egg, that's why I've made you some ham," laughed Cherry.

She took out the box of cupcakes. The smell of the orange was lovely as Cherry took the lid off the box.

"Yummy," said Freddie, "Can I have another one?"

"Yes, help yourself," said Cherry.

Once they had eaten, Freddie got his kite and his dad went off to fly it with him. It went high in the sky, floating in the wind and was really colourful.

Peaches built a sand castle and put flags on it. Cherry was throwing the ball for Nippy to catch. What a fun time they were having on this lovely sunny day!

After about an hour, the wind started to blow and the waves were crashing on the beach.

"I think we'll start getting packed up, as it's getting a little chilly," said Cherry.

They got everything back in the car and drove home, happy but a little tired. As they came up the drive, they could hear a lot of splashing coming from the garden. Peaches and Freddie ran to see what it was.

That naughty Rickster Raccoon was splashing around in their pond! Nippy came to see and started barking at him.

"Rickster, get out of our pond!" shouted Peaches.

Nippy was chasing him and finally he got out. He shook all the water off all over Nippy!

"Ha ha! that's payback for soaking us at the beach!" laughed Freddie.

Rickster ran off laughing and they all went inside to dry off. What a fun day that was!

Orange and Cranberry Cupcakes

170g margarine, 170g castor sugar, 3 eggs, 170g self-raising flour,
1 tsp baking powder, ½ tsp orange extract, the grated zest of one
orange, juice of ½ an orange,
2 oz dried cranberries coated in 2 tsp flour

Topping
150g icing sugar, juice of one orange, ½ tsp orange extract,
30-40g dried cranberries, grated rind of 1 orange

1. Mix cupcake ingredients with an electric whisk and scoop
   into cupcake cases. Bake on gas 5/190°C for 20 minutes.
2. Mix the icing sugar, orange juice (a little at a time, depending
   on the size of the orange) and orange extract together, adding
   more orange juice if needed. It should not be too runny.
3. When cool, spoon over the cupcakes and sprinkle with orange
   rind and cranberries.

Chapter 7

Summer Party

It was nearly the end of the summer holidays and every year, the Bakewells had a summer party. Cherry was in the kitchen preparing party food. She had just made a cheesecake base by putting digestive biscuits into a bag, crushing them with a rolling pin, then mixing them with mixed spice and melted butter. She pressed it into a tin and put it in the fridge to set. Freddie and Peaches were decorating the garden with dad, who was hanging bunting around the outside of the garden. Freddie and Peaches were blowing up balloons.

Nippy was also in the garden playing with the balloons.

"Nippy, stop it!" shouted Peaches. "You'll pop them!"

Once all the decorations were up, Freddie and Peaches went into the kitchen to see if Cherry needed any help.

"Hiya mummy," shouted Peaches. "Can we help?"

"Hello lovey. Yes, I'm making strawberry cheesecake."

"Oh yes!" said Freddie. "I love cheesecake!"

Cherry put icing sugar, cream cheese, double cream, Greek yoghurt, strawberries and strawberry jam on the table ready to start.

"Peaches, can you put the cream cheese, Greek yoghurt and icing sugar in the bowl please and then whisk them together?" asked Cherry.

"Okay mummy," said Peaches.

She turned on the electric whisk and blended them together with the icing sugar, making a big cloud of sugar as she mixed.

"Ooh, it looks really creamy!"

Cherry measured out the double cream and whisked it until it was fairly thick, then added it to Peaches' bowl. Peaches stirred it in. Freddie sliced some strawberries for decorating the cheesecake later. Cherry got the biscuit base out of the fridge and poured the creamy mixture in, then smoothed the top.

"There, all done, now let's put it back in the fridge to set for four hours," said Cherry.

Cherry, Freddie and Peaches went into the garden to look at the decorations.

"Oh, it looks lovely!" exclaimed Cherry. "You've done a really good job."

They had a couple of hours before guests would arrive, so they started laying the table and sorting out the drinks. The music was playing and the sun was shining. It was going to be a good party.

About three o'clock, people started arriving; Aunty Jess, Aunty Jean, cousins Charlie, Jimmy, Fran and Jo were among the guests, along with some family friends. It was going to be quite a gathering.

Cherry was hoping that Rickster Raccoon wasn't going to show up. He could smell food a mile off and he always caused trouble!

Before long, the garden was full of laughter. People were enjoying themselves and eating nice food. Then who should show up? You've guessed it, Rickster Raccoon!

He crept from behind a bush, and when nobody was looking, he started pinching sausages from the food table! He also found a box of party poppers under the table, so he sneaked in amongst the guests and started setting them off! There were screams of horror and laughter. Poor Aunty Jean dropped her drink!

"Oh Rickster, you are so naughty!" she exclaimed.

Although he was really a bit of a rascal, they had grown to love Rickster Raccoon and his mischievous behaviour!

Cherry went into the kitchen to put the strawberries on the cheesecake, warmed some jam in a saucepan and brushed it over the strawberries, then took it out into the garden, with some chocolate cake and fruit salad to hand around to the guests. The music was playing, the sun was shining and despite Rickster's naughty tricks, the party had brought everyone together.

Cherry and Jack were sitting having a drink, Freddie was eating cheesecake and Peaches was playing with Nippy. What a lovely end to the summer.

Strawberry Cheesecake

Biscuit base

225g digestive biscuits, 2 tsp mixed spice, 60g melted butter

Cheesecake filling

600g cream cheese, 130ml Greek yoghurt,

100g icing sugar, 150ml double cream,

fresh strawberries to decorate, 2 tablespoons strawberry jam

1. Put the digestive biscuits in a bag and crush with a rolling pin. Mix them with the mixed spice and melted butter, press into an 8-inch loose bottomed tin and refrigerate.
2. Whisk together the cream cheese, Greek yoghurt and icing sugar.
3. In a separate bowl, whip the cream until fairly thick and add to the cream cheese mixture. Pour into the biscuit base and return to the fridge. Leave to set for about 4 hours then decorate with fresh sliced strawberries.
4. Warm the jam in a saucepan and brush over the strawberries.

FINAL SECRET RECIPE

With Love from Cherry Bakewell

Carrot Cake

225g soft margarine, 100g castor sugar,
125g light muscovado sugar, 4 eggs, 300g self-raising flour
2 level tsp baking powder, 1 tsp ground mixed spice
1 tsp ground ginger, 1 tablespoon of milk
65g chopped pecans, 200g grated carrot

Cream cheese frosting

50g softened butter, 30g icing sugar, 200g cream cheese,
8 pecan halves for decorating, a little grated orange rind

1. Put all the cake ingredients in a bowl. Mix with an electric whisk until light and fluffy. Spoon into two 8-inch sandwich tins which have non-stick cake liners in. Bake on gas 4, 180°C for 35 minutes. Cool on a wire rack.
2. Put the softened butter and icing sugar in a bowl and mix with an electric whisk. Add the cream cheese and whisk again.
3. When the cake is cool, spread half the cream cheese frosting over the top of one cake then put the other cake on top. Spread the rest of the frosting on top of the other cake and decorate with 8 pecan halves around the outside and grate a little orange rind in the middle.

ACKNOWLEDGEMENTS

Illustrator: Lara Kerem Artwork - Facebook & Instagram

Editor: Allison Foster

Publisher: Amazon

Technical support: Damon Jones

Photography: Gary Bevan

Design support: Daniel and Paul Bevan

Karen Pritchard: For always being there

Printed in Poland
by Amazon Fulfillment
Poland Sp. z o.o., Wrocław

62813330R00033